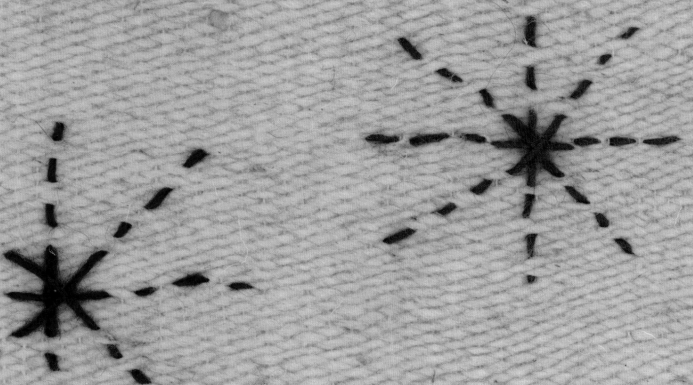
DISCARD

P9-CFB-378

BRIGHT ✦ STAR

Yuyi
Morales

NEAL PORTER BOOKS
HOLIDAY HOUSE / NEW YORK

Child,
you are
awake!

Breathe in,
then breathe out,
hermosa creatura.

You are

AL

IVE!

You are a bright star
inside our hearts.

¡Mira!

Some things you can see.

Others you must find.

So you search!

You are ready,
cosita pequeña.

Let's go!

¡Vámonos!

Oh, no!

What is that?

Look and listen.
Be alert!

corazoncito tembloroso.
Breathe in, despacito,
then gently breathe out.

Lie low.

We want you safe.

No matter where you are,
you are a bright star
inside our hearts.

And if you feel afraid

and you begin to hurt inside,

let it out.
Shout it loud!

Let the world know
what you feel!

The earth murmurs your story.
We are here to protect you.

You are
not alone.

Listen...

Sometimes

silence

tells you

secrets.

And you imagine a new story.

You imagine . . .

the most

beautiful

world.

You are a bright star

inside our hearts.

I made this book because you and I are connected, and even though that might be hard to see, it is real—real like the roots of trees and plants under the earth, sending each other signals and nourishment so that they can thrive together.

I made this book because I have many questions: When we are wronged, how do we heal? How do we care for one another when we are apart? How do we love those we don't even know?

I made this book to show you an amazing place on our planet called the borderlands, harsh and beautiful, where Mexico and the United States meet.

I made this book after Alfonso Valiente, scientist and desert expert, told me about bees, hummingbirds, bats, and other pollinators and seed-spreaders that preserve the cycle of life of plants and animals at the borderlands.

I made this book so I could bring you with me to the Sonoran Desert, where my friend Sergio Avila drove me to a "No Border Wall" camping event in New Mexico, stopping along the way at fields full of colorful grasshoppers, creosote bushes, and riparian desert oases.

I made this book to tell you the story of a whitetail fawn following her mother to find water and food, things they need to survive. But this story is about all kinds of life at the borderlands, some as tiny as the cyanobacteria, algae, and fungi that form the desert crust, and some as gigantic as a sixty-foot-tall saguaro cactus.

I made this book because at the borderlands, fences and walls have been constructed to stop people from crossing into the United States. One-hundred-year-old saguaros have been bulldozed. Paths animals regularly travel have been blocked by impenetrable barriers. These animals include Mexican gray wolves, pronghorn antelope, desert tortoises, Quino checkerspot butterflies, bighorn sheep, cactus ferruginous pygmy owls, desert pupfish, ocelots, American bison, jaguars, and many more.

I made this book because communities have been affected too. Archaeological sites, homes, and sacred places stand in the path of a border wall. The Tohono O'odham Nation, people of the desert, has lived here for many generations, yet now a security fence prevents them from crossing freely into their own land on the other side of the border.

I made this book knowing that children everywhere, but especially migrant children at the borderlands, have experienced things that they should never have to endure.

I began writing *Bright Star* in the spring of 2019. I saw how people, sometimes walking in caravans, reached the border with the hope of entering the United States. Many of these people were families with children, some were children traveling alone. Few were able to enter, and when they did, often crossing the border at places like the one you see in this book, they were detained. Families were separated and many adults were sent back to their countries of origin without their children. It is possible you saw this too. It is possible you were one of those children.

I started the final art for this book on March 13, 2020, just as the spread of the COVID-19 virus forced us into our homes. Nine months later, still in my studio, I added the final strokes of color to *Bright Star*.

I made this book using the most beautiful things I could find—words written in English and Spanish, drawings I made in my sketchbook and later refined on my computer, paper painted with bright colors, wool yarn threaded by hand and dyed with plants by weavers in the city of Oaxaca, and one ball of wool I bought at the Chamula market in Chiapas, years before I knew I would use it to make this book.

I used textures from photographs I took of things I believe should not exist, like a metal border fence and a concrete border wall in Arizona. But I also took a photograph of the arm of a baby I met with her mamá at a migrant shelter in Agua Prieta, Sonora. This I used for the color and texture of the children's skin you see in this book.

I made this book because I want you to know that no matter where you are, where you've come from, or where you are going, you should always be honored, respected, cared for, and loved.

For Octavio, with whom I sang the medicine songs that beckoned this book

And thank you to those who answered from your heart when I asked about the many things I am still learning about—solidarity, community work, and healing.

I would also like to acknowledge the following resources, organizations, and people that helped me create this book:

VIDEOS AND FILMS

Defrenne, Camille, and Suzanne Simard. "The Secret Language of Trees," TED-Ed Animations, 2019. https://ed.ted.com/lessons/the-secret-language-of-trees-camille-defrenne-and-suzanne-simard

Vilchez, Hernán. "Huicholes: The Last Peyote Guardians," Kabopro Films, 2014.

Schlyer, Krista. "Ay Mariposa," Pongo Media, 2019. https://www.aymariposafilm.com/aboutfilm

BOOKS

Schlyer, Krista. *Continental Divide: Wildlife, People, and the Border Wall.* College Station, TX: Texas A&M University Press, 2012.

Arizona-Sonora Desert Museum. *A Natural History of the Sonoran Desert.* Second ed. Berkeley, CA: University of California Press, 2015.

Chambers, Nina, Yajaira Gray, and Stephen Buchmann. *Pollinators of the Sonoran Desert: A Field Guide / Polonizadores del Desierto Sonorense: Una Guía de Campo.* Tucson, AZ: Arizona-Sonora Desert Museum, 2004.

Wiewandt, Thomas. *The Hidden Life of the Desert.* Second ed. Missoula, MT: Mountain Press, 2010.

ONLINE

Embattled Borderlands (story map) https://wildlandsnetwork.org/campaigns/borderlands/embattled-borderlands

ORGANIZATIONS

BorderLinks https://www.borderlinks.org

Nuestra Tierra Conservation Project https://www.nuestra-tierra.org

Sierra Club https://www.sierraclub.org/borderlands

Centro de Atención al Migrante Exodus, Agua Prieta, Sonora, Mexico https://www.facebook.com/camexodus

PEOPLE

Alfonso Valiente, Research Ecologist at the Biodiversity department at the Universidad Nacional Autónoma de México, Instituto de Ecología

Sergio Avila, immigrant, trail runner, biologist, who guided me into the Sonoran Desert

The Storied Studios team, including Joanna Rudnick, who accompanied me into the Sonoran Desert

Dan Millis, manager of Sierra Club's Borderlands program, with whom I toured the offices of Sierra Club and the photography exhibit *Lens on the Border*

Neal Porter Books

Text and illustrations copyright © 2021 by Yuyi Morales
All Rights Reserved
HOLIDAY HOUSE is registered in the U.S. Patent and Trademark Office.
Printed and bound in April 2021 at Toppan Leefung, DongGuan City, China.
The artwork for this book was created using acrylic paint on paper, photographed textures, digital painting, as well as weaving and embroidery.
www.holidayhouse.com
First Edition
1 3 5 7 9 10 8 6 4 2
Library of Congress Cataloging-in-Publication Data
Names: Morales, Yuyi, author, illustrator.
Title: Bright star / by Yuyi Morales.
Description: First edition. | New York : Holiday House, 2021. | "A Neal Porter Book" | Audience: Ages 3 to 7. | Audience: Grades K–1. | In English with some Spanish phrases. | Summary: "A nurturing voice reassures the lonely and afraid in difficult times"— Provided by publisher.
Identifiers: LCCN 2020044140 | ISBN 9780823443284 (hardcover)
Subjects: CYAC: Courage–Fiction.
Classification: LCC PZ7.M7881927 Br 2021 | DDC [E]—dc23
LC record available at https://lccn.loc.gov/2020044140

ISBN: 978-0-8234-4328-4 (hardcover)

This title received a 2022 Pura Belpré Youth Illustrator Honor for the U.S. English edition published by Neal Porter Books, Holiday House Publishing, Inc. in 2021. The award seal image is used with permission of the American Library Association.

DISCARD